LOVING ELORA

GINGER LEE

COPYRIGHT

Loving Elora

BY: GINGER LEE

"I'm not a moth drawn to your scorching flame. I am the lit match to your wanting wick."

~ Ginger Lee

CHAPTER 1

I ran my tongue over dry, salty lips, barely able to swallow. Water. I yearned for pure, clean water. How long had it been? Couldn't have been too long or I'd be dead already. Was I? Already gone? I couldn't see any stars but did hear wind. Must be cloudy, hiding the night sky. Shivering, I realized I was freezing in my soaking wet dress. If I was dead, I wouldn't be shivering.

A voice. I heard a faint, very deep male voice then the crunch of heavy footsteps in sand. Closer. Closer.

"Here! A girl," my salvation shouted.

I felt his body kneel beside mine. I blinked rapidly trying to focus, but the saltwater left my vision blurred. Anxiety took over my mind and I struggled to get a deep breath. Tears flowed down my cheeks into my already wet hair as I had no idea the real state I was in.

I'm sure the stranger sensed my fear. He found my ice-cold hand in the twisted material of my dress and held it tightly.

"Slow down your breathing. Try to relax. You are safe. Can you speak? Can you tell me your name?"

A second man came upon us. "Is she alive, Ash?"

"Yes, but we've got to get her warm and dry."

My first attempt failed. I pushed my voice harder only to come out as a whisper barely escaping my burning throat, "Elora."

"Asher, good god in heaven. Did she say Elora? Elora Bannon. She's the artist Mary sent for. Her ship must have wrecked! Do you see anyone else? We may need more men to search the coastline."

I squeezed his warm hand and he bent down. "I'm alone. There's no one else."

He seemed confused but didn't press me for more information. My teeth chattered. He gathered me up, wet sand and all, to carry me.

"Ben, go fetch the wagon. We'll have to come back for her trunk. There may be more of her things near," he ordered.

It was true. I was alone. I was twenty-five and had plenty of experience sailing. I almost made it to Cliff Castle's lavish dock. The surprise storm hit only a mile or so out. I should have left a day earlier so it wouldn't be dark when I arrived but my sister Lety begged to come with me. She was nineteen and full of dreams. It took longer than I expected to unload all of her belongings which she had stowed on the boat the night before my departure.

Lety practically drooled over the beautiful drawings our cousin sent to me and pleaded for an adventure. Thorpe Manor wasn't a castle, but I gave it the nickname Cliff Castle based on Mary's sketches.

I agreed to join my cousin a few months prior. Mary studied art with the accomplished Alysia Thorpe, a published illustrator under the male pen name Nathan Black. Her parents agreed to the arrangement knowing there were three wealthy Thorpe bachelors also residing in the house and Mary was of marrying age.

In a few letters, my cousin spoke affectionately about the middle brother Gideon but never disclosed the true nature of their relationship. Gideon was the one who agreed to let her send for me, an artist. I planned on staying on a few months to learn from Alysia as well.

My parents passed away when I was only ten. Lety was four. Father's sister, Aunt Rhoda, lived by the ocean in Rosarito, Mexico and took us in. Our schooling hadn't been traditional and learning from a free spirit lent itself to us running a little wild. We read all the classic books along with the scandalous ones. We swam in the ocean, painted landscapes of her twenty-acre ranch, sailed, danced, and spent nights by a bonfire on the beach telling tales from our own imaginations.

The man who I now knew as Asher Thorpe smelled of cinnamon and cloves, a combination I had a weakness for. My nose buried into his chest and I tried to tame my shaking body. I did not succeed.

The warmth of the house enveloped me as Asher stepped through the door. I also caught a whiff of sweet bread baking.

"Mr. Asher, who or what have you dragged into my kitchen," an older craggily sounding woman teased.

"Ah, Ms. Crantz, this is yet another house guest who shipwrecked on the coast and she's lucky to be alive. I don't think she's broken anything, but I'm no doctor." His tone was scolding. "We require some ladies to get her out of these clothes and into a bath. Get Liz to help."

Ms. Crantz pulled up a chair and he sat me down. I looked up, wanting to express my thanks, but my teeth were still banging together. Asher squatted in front of me, pushing my tangled hair behind trembling shoulders. Oh, his face. His beautiful face and short, dark wind-blown hair with a hint of a widow's peak. I almost drowned in the ocean and

3

now I floated away in his stormy deep blue eyes. Eyes that appeared hard and stern with thick eyebrows arched like he was scrutinizing me, like I had been a dolt to navigate my way alone. There was no doubt he was the eldest brother. At twenty-nine, maturity had started to etch three lines between his brows. He squinted a bit and only let out a deep breath. He didn't say a word and I was at a loss. The last thing I wanted was to appear pitiful. I knew I already looked very much like a drowned rodent.

With another agitated huff he stood, brushing sand from his shirt, and walked out into the hall. "All of these guests. How many more shall we have? And already causing trouble. Women!"

His tone sounded so ugly, and I bristled through the cold. How dare he act so childish! Well, I promised myself then and there to be out of his sight, determined to make damn sure he wouldn't even know I was around. Or maybe, just maybe, I would prove myself to be entirely the opposite of whatever opinion he had so quickly formed.

A girl about my age with dark auburn hair and mesmerizing aquamarine eyes entered, wrapping me in thick towels to escort me down a dimly lit hallway leading to a large washroom with a huge clawfoot tub. Hot water filled it to the brim, and I was quickly undressed and helped in. I sank down up to my chin, absorbing the steam through my nostrils.

"My name is Elizabeth, but the Thorpes call me Liz. Ash said you didn't appear to have any major injuries. If you need anything, ask for me. I'll give you some privacy. Your cousin Mary will be along shortly."

I took in a breath and submerged my whole head trying to soak the salt from my hair.

As soon as I resurfaced, a loud knock startled me, and I heard Mary's voice.

4

"Elora? May I come in?"

"Mary! Yes! Please."

I pulled my knees up somewhat covering myself as she walked in, shutting the door behind herself. She ran over and kissed my still salty head.

"I heard Ash and Ben found you. You are so lucky to be alive. You can tell me all about what happened later. Food is on its way to your room and I have a gown here. I simply require you to get several hours of sleep."

CHAPTER 2

I woke up to bright sunlight streaming through the window, feeling thoroughly drained. My head pounded. This was not how I envisioned my first day here at all. Maybe I was a complete dolt.

My first visitor was Liz, and her jaw dropped a bit making me question my decision to be brave and adventurous on my own, but at least I was in one piece. "Ma'am I think you may be sickly. Your face is as red as a raspberry."

Mary let herself in and gasped when she saw me.

"Elora! You look dreadful!"

She pulled the heavy blankets down. "You've got a fever. We'll send for Dr. Hawkins at once." She scurried out of the room.

I rolled over, away from the brightness of the sun, and told myself to accept my situation and be thankful to be alive. Mary returned with Liz who carried a basin of water and rags. I sat up, smoothing my hair as best I could. Mary thanked her with a dismissal and wiped my brow, and I shivered.

"You'll live, thank goodness, but the doctor will have to get this fever broken."

I smiled, looking at my cousin who I'd missed so much.

"I'm so happy to be here with you. I know I'll be okay. I'm afraid I haven't properly met Asher, and I'm sure I gave poor Ben a fright. Have you spoken with them since I arrived?"

She smiled. "Yes. Both were at breakfast this morning. We were all talking about you. Ben said you looked like a mermaid washed ashore. Gideon is looking forward to meeting you."

"Well, Asher didn't seem too pleased with me. I don't think he likes my being here very much." I laughed. I had to laugh or I would be angry.

"Oh, don't mind him, he's an old grump. I've only seen him smile a handful of times when he's teasing Gideon or Ben. He hasn't been happy since…"

Mary's voice faded and she silenced herself as if she was about to tell a secret.

She knew I realized. "Never mind. Elora, we are glad you are here. Alysia loves teaching and--"

I interrupted, "What happened? Why is he unhappy? You know I won't tell a soul."

She put the basin on the floor and sat by my side again. "Asher was engaged. Her name was March Andrews. Her family has a vineyard near the border of the Thorpe property. They met at a party and he was smitten. Of course, I learned this from Gideon because March passed away two years ago from influenza. Gideon said Asher grew cold after. I don't blame him. I can't imagine."

Mary jumped up, ready to change the subject. "I will get your soup. You need something in your belly. Dr. Hawkins should be here this afternoon"

❦

I still sat sweating and chilled after eating lunch and reading the Union-Tribune. Mary knocked on the door. "Here's the doc, as ordered."

The man strode in, and a large, beautiful hand extended towards mine and I took it. "Hello, Ma'am, Dr. Cameron Hawkins. It is a pleasure to meet you. I'm sorry you aren't feeling well. I hear you were sailing your own boat from Rosarito? Alone?"

Oh no. He wanted to scold me too. I opened my mouth to defend myself, but he continued.

"I'm impressed! Not many women would know their way around a sailboat. And you almost made it successfully."

My goodness. He was handsome. Did every man in San Diego turn the ladies' heads? I didn't think he would be so close to my age. Tall, lean, and muscled under his suit and white shirt with short blond hair and light green eyes that lit up when he walked in the room. I might have been a little smitten.

"I appreciate your kind words, sir. My aunt taught me everything I know. She is a very independent woman. Thank you for traveling here to see to my fever."

"Please, call me Cameron. I believe a woman should have as much knowledge about survival and the world as a man. I know Alysia and I am so proud of what she has accomplished. One day she will be able to illustrate under her own name. Now, let's take a look at you."

"May I?" he asked, and I nodded as he pulled the blankets down. I was covered by my white gown. He felt my head and pulled a stethoscope from his bag. He sat on the edge of the bed and placed it over my heart. Embarrassment from knowing he heard my rapid pulse rate would have reddened my cheeks if they weren't already flushed from fever.

"Take a deep breath. Another. Sit forward."

He placed it on my upper back, over one lung, then the other. I read all of the anatomy books on my aunt's bookshelves and poured over the pictures many times, so I understood his methods.

"Your lungs sound strong and clear. Any cuts or scrapes from the accident? There are rocky areas on the shoreline." I shook my head no. He replaced the stethoscope and retrieved a brown bottle. "This is Aspirin or acetylsalicylic acid. I want you to take one every four hours around the clock. There will be plenty left for use later. Aspirin works on headaches, body aches, and monthly pains. I will stay here until the fever breaks. It shouldn't take more than a couple of days. Tomorrow morning after I check on you, we will go out for a short walk to get you some fresh air."

"I promise to be a good patient. Thank you, again."

He smiled. "Like I said, I'm very happy to be of service, Ma'am." His eyes lingered a moment before he left the room.

Mary stayed, handing me the glass of water and a white tablet. "My my. I believe you've made quite the impression on Dr. Hawkins. He simply couldn't stop smiling."

She beamed as I swallowed the bitter pill.

"And I look dreadful." We laughed.

"You are a natural beauty, Elora. You just haven't been around high society much. There are dinner parties and dances to attend with rich families like the Marstons and Spreckels. We shall make art during the day and dance all night." She twirled around the room. "Oh, most of your things are clean and dry now. I'll have them brought up. Want a bath?"

"Oh, yes. And I promise I will take it easy, but I wish I could sit and read a book in the library. Maybe open a window, let the night air in?"

"That would be lovely. I'll be back after you get cleaned up."

CHAPTER 3

*M*y trunk sat at the foot of the bed when I returned from the bath. The wardrobe door stood open and my dresses were hanging and appeared pristine. Feeling the lush velvet and satin, I thanked the heavens they survived. My box! I spied my beloved jewelry box and the key next to it on the dresser. My heart skipped a beat. Mother's pearls and brooches were safe. A simple, pale blue, cotton day dress would be just fine for a visit to the library. I pulled my hair up in a wispy chignon and Mary joined me in the hallway.

Her long, burgundy, satin skirt swished as we made our way down the mahogany staircase. She kept my hand in the crook of her arm in case I got lightheaded.

A window stood open between two massive bookcases standing across from the doorway. Brown leather sofas were situated facing each other, encouraging ripe conversation or debate. Candles glowed atop card tables to the left of the room and a rather large fireplace hissed and crackled on the right. Planted, staring into the flames, was Asher Thorpe. I hadn't seen him since he rescued me. Carved faces of dragons with spread wings and long twisting tails on the mantle framed his tall, flawless body.

He turned with no emotion on his face. I nodded, as did he. Mary scurried over and slid a small chair in front of the window.

"I have to choose a book first, Mary."

"Oh, yes. Mr. Thorpe has the most beautiful Bibles."

"May I suggest one," Asher spoke up. He went to the bookcase, scanned a row with a long finger, and plucked his suggestion from the shelf. He held up *The Wonderful Wizard of Oz*. "I think Ms. Bannon would prefer something a little more whimsical."

The offer surprised me. I sat down by the billowing white curtain and he handed me the book. "Thank you." He gave a brief smile and returned to the fire.

Mary chose a red leather-bound Bible and sat on the nearest sofa. Gideon and Ben strode in laughing, ready for a late-night card game, and Asher joined them. My chair sat facing them and I couldn't help but observe. I grew up with all females and there seemed to be something special about the camaraderie of brothers. They would argue and laugh hysterically in the same breath. Asher played along but kept wearing a serious face. Ben's brown curls bounced across his brows as he made silly faces in my direction. He, the youngest, enjoyed being the center of attention as did my little sister Lety. She would absolutely swoon over Ben. I missed her in that moment.

Gideon and Mary shook heads at each other like they were sharing unspoken thoughts. I could tell he liked her, but how much? I wasn't sure. My thoughts were definitely not on the book in my hands, so I shut it and gazed out of the window. The crisp air filled my lungs and a chill swept over my skin. Liz came in and served what appeared to be whiskey to the men. She lingered near Asher a little longer than the others, but he didn't seem to notice. Her tray also held a glass of water and the brown bottle Dr. Hawkins left in my room.

"Ma'am." I took the pill and emptied the entire glass.

"Good! Water is important. We must keep you hydrated." Cameron clasped his hands together as he seemingly floated in from the hall and directly to me. His face appeared genuine and happy. The back of his hand touched my forehead. "Chilled a bit?" He noticed the gooseflesh on my arms and led me to stand next to the warmth of the fire, keeping his hand on my elbow.

"I had to escape my room for a while, but I plan on turning in soon."

"You cannot forget our walk after breakfast." He winked and the fire danced in his eyes as he placed me back on the chair with a thrill of excitement running through me.

Mary gave me a knowing look and I laughed. Asher did not seem amused and scowled at his drink. Oh, to know what he was thinking.

❦

I thought I could stay away. After holding that familiar female form in my arms, her nose nestling into my shirt...who was I kidding? I ached for my March. God, I missed her.

Elora Bannon made my bored black heart rattle the walls of my rib cage. I hadn't felt that inspired rush of blood in a long while. Seeing her seated in the library, the night air chilling her skin had me cursing myself for wanting to take that full pout of a bottom lip between my teeth.

CHAPTER 4

*T*he next morning at breakfast Ben sat by my side excitedly asking all about me. Having just turned twenty, his youthfulness was bubbly and sweet and I could tell we would be good friends. I couldn't wait to write to Lety about him. Asher and Gideon had joined us at the long table in the middle of it all, but Asher only listened. I felt his eyes on me and glanced his way a few times. He proved to be a tough nut to crack, and I wondered if he had any kind of relationship with Liz. I decided Mary and Gideon may need a little help in the area of romance. Both were too shy for their own good. Sooner or later one of them would have to take control or they would only run circles around each other for eternity.

Asher finally spoke. "Has anyone seen the good doctor this morning?"

"He was up before the sun, ate very early, and went out for a run. I saw him out on the beach. I couldn't sleep so I went out for a walk myself," Gideon replied.

"We have to go for another swim before it gets too cold," Ben added.

On the other side of me, Mary patted my thigh. "I bet you swim in the ocean all the time, don't you?"

"Yes. Lots. I love the ocean. I don't think I could ever move away from it."

"It does have a way of soothing the soul and mind. And the smell…"

We were all surprised by Asher's poetic sentiments. It was almost like he had forgotten where he was for a moment, but then realized, cleared his throat, and got up to leave.

"See you all later." He nodded and walked away.

Ben let out a laugh. "Ash does love the ocean. He seems the city type, but he always comes back."

I pondered what that meant. Always comes back. Like he often took a fancy to leaving. I had heard of men who escaped to the city for fun and maybe a frolic or two. Men with wives even. Big cities enticed with saloons, games, and women.

Dr. Hawkins entered with damp hair and finely dressed, wearing his smile. He came to stand next to me and offered his hand. "Are you feeling up for our walk this morning Ms. Bannon?"

I took his help up from my chair and he boldly tucked my hand over his elbow. I nodded and politely asked if anyone wished to join us. They all declined, and Mary gave me the naughtiest look. I prayed the doctor missed it.

❦

*H*e steered us toward the gardens instead of the beach. The gardens felt more secluded with high walls and bushes. Cameron looked down at me as we walked. "I must admit I'm sad to say your fever is gone. You look very well, Elora. I hope our paths will cross again soon.

16

There is a dance this weekend. Will the Thorpes be in attendance? They usually are."

This was the first I had heard of it, but with my being sick, Mary hadn't elaborated further on the promised all night dancing. "I'm not sure. I will have to ask Mary. Will you be there?"

"Oh yes. I love to dance with beautiful women, and if you're not there it just won't be as fun."

I blushed and looked down at our feet. God, the man was bold and equally as charming. The women probably lined up to dance with the bachelor doctor.

"Well, if I do attend, I might save a dance for you," I flirted. I knew I flirted, and I shouldn't, but he made it easy and he started it.

"Might?" He stopped and turned toward me. I just looked up at him, parting my lips, wondering what in the world he was going to say. "Elora Bannon, I'm counting on it." His serious look was new. Not the beaming smile I was used to. He leaned in and brushed the smallest hint of his warm mouth to my forehead. It had me tingling and shocked at the same time. Bold indeed.

I stammered a bit but wanted to seem in control of my emotions. "Well, doctor, we better get back. I don't wish to relapse and cause you any more trouble." He followed close behind, not adding any further conversation until he bid me a simple goodbye at the steps to the house.

❦

I hurried to find Mary who was already in the drawing room, standing in front of an easel with Alysia. I rolled my eyes at her.

"Elora, tell me all about it. Did Dr. Hawkins behave?" When it took me a moment to answer as I bit my lip and fiddled with my paint brushes, her eyes grew wide. She and Alysia were intrigued. "Well, out with it!"

"He said I seemed well, inquired about a dance this weekend and would like me to save him a dance…and then he kissed my forehead."

Alysia gasped and shook her head. "Oh, dear. You have already cast your spell. Our days and nights are about to get exciting around here," she laughed. "Every single girl is after that man. Well, Asher is in the running too but he's not very approachable and that mood of his. Liz is holding out hope he will look her way, but I'm not sure her heart is in the right place." She shook her head again.

"So, why aren't you interested in Dr. Hawkins?"

"I'm seeing a wonderful man. Blaine Black."

I mentally made the connection.

"He made it possible for my work to be published. He is co-owner of the publishing company and in print I pose as Nathan Black, his brother. It works out quite well because he is very easy on the eyes, and he cares about me a great deal. We simply adore each other."

"That's so lovely," Mary swooned.

Alysia spoke her mind. "Mary, you better get your hooks into Gideon, or another woman will. You know he likes you and you know he doesn't express his feelings very well."

Mary whined a bit, "But I don't either. And besides, a woman wants to be chased a little, doesn't she? Maybe you should be lecturing Gideon instead of me."

I interjected on the subject. "You could flirt a little more. Prance around a little more. Pull that desire to the surface. Make it known you wish to be wooed."

Alysia looked at me in amazement. "You should try writing some poetry. And how do you know so much about getting a man's attention?"

"I promise I'm no harlot, but I have read a great many

books, and some were not so chaste. Also, I believe I'm coming to the age where you naturally develop more…wants and needs." I looked down at my hands.

"You speak the truth. Men aren't the only beings who have needs." Alysia sounded like she had much more experience than Mary or me.

Somewhere during our conversation, we had all started painting. A beach landscape formed on my canvas. I had never been the best artist, but maybe Alysia would teach me a thing or two. I had never thought about writing either, but why not give it a go?

❧

*S*ometime later, Ben poked his ruffled head into the room. "Ladies, lunch will be served shortly." He walked in and stood next to me. "Not bad for a novice," he joked. He smelled of the salty air.

I laughed and elbowed him in the ribs. "Hey now, maybe it is a bit abstract." We both tilted our heads sideways and laughed again.

CHAPTER 5

*S*eeing senior Mr. Thorpe seated at the table was a nice surprise. Mrs. Thorpe had been ill for a while and almost never left her room. He spoke loudly but pleasantly. "Ms. Bannon, I haven't welcomed you properly. We are delighted to have you here with us. If you need anything, don't hesitate to tell my sons and they will see to it."

Asher, who was seated next to his father, choked a bit on his tea. No telling what he was thinking.

"There is one thing. I would like to borrow or purchase a blank journal from your library. I noticed a few on the shelf."

"Oh, certainly. Take one and get a nice pen from the drawer of my desk."

"Thank you, Mr. Thorpe. You're so kind."

Asher was about to take leave when he stopped at the door and leaned on the jam. "Ms. Bannon, can I show you to the library and I will fetch you a pen?"

It was me almost choking now but I fought it back, and the others looked blankly at me like they were watching a play and wondered what was to happen in the next scene.

"Of course." He started walking and I jumped up and followed him down the hall.

✣

I loved the library, and it was so different during the day with the sun shining through the windows. The lack of a fire in the fireplace lent the room to smell of books instead of burning wood and cinder. Asher went to the desk and I took a blue leather-bound journal out of the stack. Blue was my favorite color. Like the ocean. Much like Asher Thorpe's eyes, but this was darker. More navy. He wasn't speaking so I did.

"I have read a little of the book you suggested. I like it very much."

He only said, "I knew you'd prefer it."

He handed me a silver pen and I expected him to excuse himself, but he stayed near me. The pen felt cool in my palm. "Gorgeous," I said.

"Indeed." His eyes traveled from my head to my toes, and I turned hot. I changed the subject quickly.

"How is your mother? I don't see the family spending much time with her."

He didn't move away and seemed to lean a margin closer. My breath escalated.

"She sleeps a lot. We don't want to disturb her. I do miss her. She used to sit in here and watch us play cards when we were young." Asher pried the journal from my white knuckles and flipped through the blank pages. "What will you write?"

I swallowed hard. "Oh, about my time here, I suppose. Alysia thinks I could be a good writer because I have a big imagination. I might sketch a bit, too."

"Will Cameron end up in your book?"

I stared, not knowing how to respond. My body was responding to Asher leaning even nearer. His nose skimmed my cheek and he placed his wide mouth on mine. It was only a taste. A sample. It was warm and sweet and made me want more. My fingers wanted to drop the pen and tangle in his hair, but I refrained. My eyes were still closed as his lips left mine.

"Maybe I'll be in there too," he growled and left me in a haze of pure sensuality. He clearly knew how to play the game of seduction, and he would almost certainly end up in my journal. I would have to take care to hide it too, because he would be one to read it and celebrate his victory.

❧

I sat on the couch and began to write of my terrible arrival to Dr. Hawkins to Asher Thorpe. Mary finally found me almost two hours later. "What on earth are you doing? I was sketching and the time passed by without noticing. Then I looked around and remembered the last time I saw you you were heading here with Ash."

I feigned innocence, "He gave me a pen. I wanted to get my thoughts down. Is it already dinner time?"

"Yes, I guess in about a half hour."

My eyes gleamed with mischief. "I want you to wear one of my dresses to dinner and I'll pull your hair up."

"What is up your sneaky sleeve?"

"Nothing at all. Just a little seducing."

Mary laughed as I pulled her to her room.

❧

I wore a fine red velvet dress with fitted sleeves to my elbow. It clung to the curve of my hips a bit and the neckline was not too revealing but dipped below my collar bones. I adorned Mary in romantic wine velvet. The shape mimicked my dress and pearls accentuated our exposed necks. Maybe I did know how to pull it off. We would have Gideon falling at my cousin's feet in no time. And Asher. Asher was dark and mysterious, and I wanted to know more.

CHAPTER 6

$\mathcal{I}$t being Friday, the table was set for a more formal evening. Candlesticks perched like seagulls on a dune, flickered along the middle, still not obscuring the glimmer in the eyes of the dinner guests. We all quickly became heady from the wine which was served by Liz who wore an especially revealing frock that gave a risqué show of her bosom every time she bent at the waist to pour more drink into each goblet.

I was pleased to meet Blaine Black who was so close to Alysia their knees touched. His hand rested on the back of her neck and he toyed with her hairline. She squirmed when it tickled. The scene was fairly arousing, and I could tell Asher, who sat next to Blaine, tried not to watch the couple or Liz on full display. I couldn't keep my eyes off of them. Being that lustful must feel spectacular. Meanwhile, next to me, Gideon couldn't keep his eyes off Mary. Just as I had planned. She could flirt very well when she played the part and the plentiful drink only aided in lowering inhibitions. Asher spoke across the table to Ben, on my other side.

"I'm not playing cards tonight. I need some air." He gave

me a glance and scooted his chair back. I felt disappointment when he tossed his linen napkin on the table and left out abruptly. I wanted to flirt and have fun with everyone without being with fever like I was last time. As the guests made their way to the library, I stopped in the parlor to look out of the huge back windows leading to the portico. The tip of a cigarette glowed and bobbed as Asher walked the coastline and out of sight. Liz walked in but hesitated like she was surprised to see me there, then turned and left. I wondered if she thought about going to find Asher but didn't want me to see.

*M*y intrigue got the best of me, and I slipped out and trailed behind him. I felt like he knew I was there, and he affirmed it when he climbed up on a rock and thrust out his hand to help me up. He didn't talk, didn't ask why I came. He only flicked the butt down to the sand below and kept his eyes forward.

The ocean pitched and rolled, mirroring my inner turmoil. I lay stretched out on the large flat rock. Asher squatted beside me still saying nothing. The sky darkened quickly as clouds blanketed the moon and stars. He took out another cigarette, lit it, and pulled in a puff. I could take the silence no longer. My want burned in my belly. I sat up and plucked it from his lips to get a better smell. "Mmm cloves. I love the scent of cloves."

He nodded. "Yes. Tasty too. Just take a little into your mouth, hold it there, and blow it out." I did as he said with ease then took a bigger puff, tilting my face to the stars and expelling a thin, slow stream of smoke.

I felt Archer's eyes move from my lips down to my neck. I

giggled. "I feel like a dragon." A deep laugh escaped his chest. A first from him.

"You aren't a witch, or something are you?"

In return I let out a witchy laugh. "Oh, Mr. Thorpe, what if I was? A witch? Gypsy? Voodoo priestess? A fortune teller?" His face was serious now, contemplating the possibilities. I laughed again. "No, I am none of those things." I held out the cigarette and Asher closed his hand over mine, sliding it from my fingers. His face went dark with desire.

I felt it down to my marrow and decided to test the waters by being a little suggestive. "Women aren't supposed to smoke, but I find it exciting to break the rules."

Asher scanned the waves. "We can come out here and smoke any time. No one will know. I won't tell anyone." There were other things I imagined doing with him out here alone. My mind swirled with questions about he and Liz. Did he meet her here? Did he share his seemingly alone time with her? My heart hoped not. He was so like the sea. I felt a connection to this moody man as I did the moody sea. He put out the last bit of the cigarette on the rocky ground and stood. The wind blew the tails of his coat. He looked like a painting.

Asher turned to me and held out a hand. "Why don't we head back to the house. It's getting chilly and the wind is picking up." I gave him my hand and found myself pulled swiftly against his chest, his eager mouth crushing mine. It happened so fast and his tongue so skillful I didn't fight it. Asher's arms went around my waist and I never wanted him to let go. His hands burned through my dress and I had never felt such lust. We slowly came to a stop and our lips remained only a breath away. Two bodies so close, forming one shadow.

I felt his smirk as he whispered gruffly, "I'm sorry. I wanted to taste you again and I usually do what I want." I knew he wished to take things further and I knew I would eventually give in, but I would not be so easy a conquest. Stolen kisses would have to appease him for now.

He kept my hand until we reached the portico at the rear of the manor. "You know your way back to your room?"

"Yes, of course."

&

I drifted off to sleep thinking of Asher Thorpe's delightful mouth and woke in the morning craving a clove cigarette.

CHAPTER 7

*N*one of the brothers were at breakfast. Mary and I occupied ourselves in the drawing room with Alysia for the entire day. She spent her time sketching out the gardens of Thorpe Manor while I painted a nightscape. My inappropriate thoughts kept me from making any progress and Alysia could tell my mind dwelled elsewhere.

"Are you thinking about your promised dance with Dr. Hawkins tonight?"

"Promised? I never promised…but I will dance with him." We all laughed.

Mary started washing her paint brushes. "We need to get ready in a little bit. I'll go have our bath water prepared."

❦

A dance. At a fancy neighboring mansion. At none other than the Andrews' vineyard and estate as Mary informed me while we dressed.

"Oh, it's beautiful. Kind of like an Italian villa. Very romantic."

She and Gideon had turned a page since dinner the night before and she couldn't wait to twirl around the room in his arms.

I knew I would be in the illustrious company of Dr. Hawkins, but my high spirits fell when Mary said Asher most certainly would not be going. He had never returned to the Andrews' estate after March's death.

❦

*W*hat the hell was I doing? I had attended the occasional business dinner, but it had been two long years since I had stepped foot near a dance floor. And I never intended to go near the Andrews' again, but there was no way in hell I was going to let Elora Bannon traipse off and spend the evening floating around in another man's arms.

Gideon came into my room astonished to see me wearing a suit. "Well, I'll be damned. Asher Thorpe. What has gotten into you, or should I say who?"

I gave him a knowing scowl. "Gideon, I need you to grow some and formally ask Mary to accompany you. You two will be riding in my car and you are to bring Elora along."

"Ah. There's the truth of it. I think I can manage that. Mary and I had a nice time last night. Very nice, indeed."

"You held hands?" I asked as sarcastically as I could.

"Ash. I think I gave her her first real kiss. She moaned."

He dragged out the word for more impact and I laughed. "Well, it's about time, you scoundrel."

"What about you and Elora? It's a bit fast isn't it? I mean, you haven't…"

"I know. Believe me. I know."

❦

*M*ary and I met Gideon and the others near the front door, and he took her hand assessing her deep purple satin dress. "Mary, I wanted to ask you if you would accompany me to the dance?"

My heart overflowed for her as she bounced up and down. "Oh, yes! I'd love to."

"We are riding with Ash. Elora will ride with us, of course."

I couldn't believe it, and neither could anyone else who heard what Gideon had said.

Ben perked up. "Asher is actually going? To the dance? At the Andrews?"

Gideon winked. "Apparently."

❧

*N*one of us saw Asher leave the house, but he was waiting outside with his rumbling black Peerless Model 27. It sat beside their father's automobile ready to go. Ben drove Alysia and Blaine.

He hopped out of his driver's seat and opened the doors. Asher's blue eyes mirrored the blue silk of my dress, and he showed Gideon and Mary to the back seat then walked me around to the seat next to his.

He whispered near my ear, "You look stunning," and helped me in.

The Peerless was my first car ride. My gloved hands skimmed the tufted red leather seats. My thoughts were on Asher and how he must feel coming to this house again. Surely, he would know Mary and I talked, and I wanted to make sure he was alright. The journey there didn't take long. We pulled up to the front and Asher helped me out, then the others. A young boy about fourteen or fifteen parked the car.

❧

*T*he crowd was large, and the bodies mingled so close. Excitement filled the air. A small orchestra played lively music and dancers twirled in unison.

Gideon led our group straight to the refreshments. "We should drink some wine first. Elora hasn't had any Andrews' wine. It's the best in the nation."

It was the best I'd ever tasted. I consumed the entire goblet too fast. My head spun a bit. Then I spied someone making his way over.

"Dr. Hawkins." I tipped my head to him cordially.

He boldly took my hand and wrapped it around his arm again. "Ms. Bannon, I told you to call me Cameron. Let's have that dance, shall we?"

He sent a smug smile to Asher. I looked back over my shoulder, being pulled to the floor as Asher downed his wine in one gulp.

❧

*C*ameron turned me to face him as the music slowed. He made me feel uncomfortable but surprised me by barely touching my waist and hardly holding my hand. It felt a little too proper. I found it hard to follow his lead being so loosely held.

"You don't know how happy I am that you are here, Elora. I've been waiting for you. I haven't danced with anyone else."

"Well, Cameron, you shouldn't have waited. I plan on dancing with the others and so should you. Don't miss out on dancing with all of the beautiful women."

"I don't want any of the other beautiful women."

His look was absolutely devilish. Now I began to get an

idea of why he was still a bachelor. Maybe once he got close, his demons came out to play. The song ended and I desperately felt the need to get away. His hand clamped down on my waist as if to hold me in place. "I expect another dance." And with that, he let go.

CHAPTER 8

I was rattled and I knew Asher could tell. He sat at a table drinking more wine, watching me make my way to him. My hands shook a little as I tried to steady them. Asher pushed away from the table and took my elbow.

"My turn. Leave your gloves on the table."

I had no idea why, but I did as he said and slid them off. I didn't feel tense with Asher. Just the sound of his voice helped put me at ease. He held my waist with a large, firm hand, and he watched my slender fingers fold around the other.

"Why did you want me to take off my gloves?"

"Because I want to feel your skin against mine."

I swooned. I swooned hard and fast and my head buzzed from more than just wine. My goodness, this man and the smolder he emitted. Thank heavens the song was somewhat upbeat, and we glided easily together. Asher even smiled and I giggled. On a turn I caught Cameron frowning at us. It was the first time I had seen him frown and I got edgy again.

"El, what's wrong?"

My mouth curved up at the sound of that. El. Like an

endearment. "It's Cameron. I don't want to sound full of myself, but I'm afraid he may be too enthused about our friendship. He actually frightened me. Just a little. Nothing I can't handle. Don't think a thing about it."

"Frightened?" He searched my face, his serious. "I have the feeling you can take care of yourself but promise me you won't get caught alone with him."

"Oh, I don't plan on it. He's not like you."

"What do you mean?"

"Well, you're…you're passionate and real. I can tell. I feel safe with you. He's conniving and likes to be in complete control."

"Can I show you something? We would be alone…"

"Yes. I trust you."

§.

*A*sher led me pretty far down a dimly lit hall, passing several doors. We stopped in front of one, and he took out a key from his coat pocket to unlock it. He spoke low, "It's okay. I asked Mr. Andrews if I could come to his office. We've known each other a long time."

We stepped in and he locked the door again. The room smelled of pipe tobacco and beautiful dark wood covered every surface, floor to ceiling. There was a large desk and at least six bookcases. Asher led me behind the desk and pulled back a black curtain to reveal a huge oil painting.

"*The Fall of the Damned*," I marveled.

To see it up close. Every detail, every stroke, made me giddy. "Oh, Ash."

He stayed behind me, hands rubbing down my arms, fingers finding mine, lacing them together.

"I know how much you love art. I had to show you. It

wasn't easy for me coming here tonight, but this makes it worth it."

I kept his fingers intertwined with mine and pulled his arms around my waist. His chest pressed against my back and he was so warm. His breath fluttering across my neck made me suck in air. Asher's lips touched my bare shoulder, and I went weak. I let go of one of his hands and reached to grasp the curls on the back of his head, keeping his mouth in place as he sucked my sensitive skin. My body instinctively arched, and I felt him hard on my backside. I turned around and covered that hot mouth with mine. I let my tongue slip between his lips, and he groaned and teased with his. My desire became too much, and I knew it had to be painful for him. I reluctantly pushed back a little, leaving my hands on his chest. Our hearts pounded, breaths ragged. He kept his forehead on mine.

"El...was that...was that okay?"

I smiled, much like a greedy child. "Yes."

He sat down in the large desk chair and pulled me onto his lap facing the masterpiece. "Thank you for bringing me to see this. It's magnificent. And thank you for coming out tonight. Mary said you wouldn't."

"And you know why?"

"Yes. It must be difficult."

"It is, but I came because of you. I wouldn't have come for any other reason. We should get back, I guess."

He sighed and pushed me up from his lap. He locked the office door again, and we joined the party once more.

੬ક

*W*e played coy, each entering the packed room separately. Asher went first while I stopped in the washroom to wet my flushed face with cool water.

Ben found me as soon as I returned and pulled me to dance again. He was the happiest human I had ever met.

"Asher told me to dance with you. Not that I didn't want to."

"Oh, he did?"

"He's jealous, you know?"

"Of whom?"

"Every other hot-blooded man here. Hell, he's probably watching us now with envy that I'm holding on to you and he's not."

"Ben, you have a way with words. And you flatter me. I am glad you're so easy to talk to. You speak your mind and I like that."

"Okay, well, to tell you the truth…I'm jealous of Asher."

We stilled the dancing a bit. "Ben."

"I know. I know. I would never. I still want us to be friends."

"Me too."

Ben's eyes went jovial again. "Snacks! Let's get snacks and go sit with Ash."

The night kept going. Mary wasn't kidding. It seemed it would never end. Almost no one had left to go home. I couldn't fathom how the orchestra kept up. Between the three Thorpe brothers, I had managed to keep away from Cameron and I was glad. Even if he got his claws into me at this point, I was too tired to move. I propped up my throbbing head on my fist and rubbed my temple with my fingers. Asher had been dancing with Alysia and returned to the seat next to mine. He looked concerned when I grimaced a bit.

"El, are you okay?"

"Just a headache is all. So, how long does the party last?"

He gently touched my back. "I'll get the car."

He stood and I grabbed his arm. "Everyone won't fit into the other car. I'll be alright."

Asher had already wagged a finger at Gideon who made his way to us with Mary in tow. "Elora doesn't feel well. I'd like to take her home."

Mary insisted, "Oh, I'm ready to leave. I'm about to pass out."

❦

*I*t was well past midnight when we reached the manor. My heels were killing my feet and I slipped them off. When Asher opened the car door, he noticed I was now barefoot and scooped me up to carry me over the rocky ground. I didn't protest at all. I was so grateful to not be in my heels. He sat me back down before the four of us went inside.

"I just want to get out of this dress and into bed," I groaned.

"Any bed?" Asher asked with that wide mouth cocked in a grin, only half joking. He grabbed me and squeezed me in a hug.

Lord, he could heat me up quick. He let go and I already missed his hard chest. He spoke to Gideon and Mary, "Thank you for getting me out."

Mary tugged me down the hall and up the stairs to our rooms where I stripped down and didn't bother with a night gown. The blankets felt heavenly against my naked body, and I slept like a baby.

CHAPTER 9

*B*ack home on Sundays, I was used to swimming in the ocean. I woke up early, pulled on a thick shift and a navy-blue robe. Out of my window, I could see waves tenderly lapping the sand like a gentle lover. The sun pinkened the sky with its first offerings of light. The creak of my door made the only noise besides the big ticking clock that guarded the end of the hall. My slippers silently padded downstairs and out onto the portico. After smelling the ocean air, I got a little wild and started running through the sand where I kicked off my shoes and tossed my robe to the ground. The sun shone brighter, and I treasured the warmth on my face. Pulling my shift up over my knees, I skipped out into the water, then I noticed movement to my left.

❧

I let out a scream and sank down so the waves covered me up to my shoulders while Asher, Gideon, and Ben laughed at my expense. I instinctively crossed my arms over my breasts. The three men wore nothing but cotton underpants that hung low on their hips and laid wet and snug over every other part. I couldn't believe they kept running and playing in plain sight. Why did they not own proper bathing suits? I rolled my eyes at them and swore under my breath for being so feral in front of them.

Asher's tan chest reflected the sun, and he slowly waded waist deep towards me where I remained somewhat concealed. Water dripped from his dark hair and he looked delicious. The smile on his face was not reassuring me that he would behave. When he came near, his body went lower and he swam around me like a seal gliding fluidly. I had to turn round and round to keep my eyes on him. He suddenly morphed into a shark circling his prey. The shift began to wind around my legs, and I bobbled, causing me to release my arms from my own shoulders to keep afloat.

Gideon and Ben weren't paying us any attention. Asher finally stopped stalking me and kept at arms-length. "Good morning, El." He grinned.

I huffed, "Morning, Ash."

"I'm sorry we gave you a scare. Deeply sorry." His hand went to his heart, but he teased. "It is a beautiful day for swimming. Do you wear a bundlesome shift when you swim at home?"

"No, actually." I lifted my chin in the air. "Not a stitch."

I could tell his brain worked around my words. "In fact, my favorite is a good…naked…midnight dip."

"Elllll…you, temptress."

He kicked once, closing the space between us, and I pushed off the sandy bottom with both feet propelling me in the direction of the shore. I laughed but heard him splashing close behind me as I frantically fought the wet cloth slowing me down. I had made it so close, the waves hitting the back of my calves when Asher grabbed me from behind and swung me off my feet. He twirled me around and placed my feet back on the sand but kept a hold of me. I felt every muscle and bodily organ the man possessed pressed against me. His nose nuzzled my hair.

"Ash. I need my robe."

"Oh, alright." He kept an arm around my shoulders as we went to retrieve it and acted a complete gentleman, not looking down at the soaked silhouette of my very visible breasts. He picked it up and shook out the sand.

I tied it around myself and kept my eyes on his. He made no attempt to cover himself. He pushed a salty tangle from my face and tucked it behind my ear. "Do you remember the night I found you, my mermaid?"

I warmed at his words as he licked the salt from his lips, but teased him, "I remember how much joy it brought you to have, what was it? Another house guest and already causing trouble?"

The other brothers were already out of the water and sprawled out drying in the sun. Asher gestured toward them. "I can rein them in and you stay. Have a relaxing time. I'll ask Mary and Alysia to join you."

"Sounds nice." I knew Gideon and Ben had their eyes closed so I went up on tiptoes and kissed Asher long and hard and he immediately got aroused. "I couldn't help myself. Do I tempt you?"

"Yes, woman. Very much so. I'll deal with you later." He kissed my forehead and called out, "Boys, let's go. Leave the lady be. We've had our fun."

I watched them go and I lay out in the sun.

§

I didn't hear the end of it on the walk back to the manor. Ben said what was on his mind, of course. "You know she saw all of us practically naked."

"Yes, I am well aware."

"And after seeing what we each have to offer she probably prefers me now." Ben joked but started running as soon as the words left his mouth and I dashed after him, not catching up on purpose. I didn't feel like wrestling at the moment. I was still thinking about that kiss and El's wet body. And that wasn't all. Her free spirit and the fact that she would race out into the ocean without a care gripped me passionately. She fit. She felt right and it scared the hell out of me.

❧

*W*e spent most of the morning and afternoon on the beach. I wrote in my journal and took a nap before dinner. Sunday naps were my favorite.

CHAPTER 10

I snapped awake the instant I felt the mattress sink next to my side and something hard prop against my leg. Asher's large warm hand went across my mouth to silence any protest, not that I wanted to.

"It's me." He lifted his hand and held the headboard as I scooted to sitting, pulling the covers up to my chin.

"Well, I know it's you, but what are you doing in my room sitting on my bed?"

"Your door was open, and you slept so sweet. I couldn't resist. Sorry I woke you." I hadn't remembered leaving my door open. He played with the loose ends of my hair, which I had pulled into a bun. The hard something was Asher's thigh and it rested against mine comfortably. He appeared already dressed for dinner. No one was in the hall, so he took my hand and laced our fingers together again. It only made me want them all over me. I secretly wished the door was closed, but that would indeed be scandalous.

"Have you been writing in your journal?"

"Yes."

"Anything about the grumpy oldest Thorpe brother?"

"Maybe," I teased. "I have to write to Lety tomorrow. She's probably dying to hear about Cliff Castle."

"Cliff Castle? What's Cliff Castle?"

"Oh, it's silly really. I called this house Cliff Castle because Mary sent me lovely sketches and Thorpe manor looked just like a castle sitting on a cliff. The name stuck with Lety. She fantasizes about everything."

"So, she has a big imagination like her older sister. What do you fantasize about?" The tone of his voice dropped low and hummed in my ear. My body instantly responded.

"I dare not say." No, certainly not. Asher would dash to the door and lock it if I uttered one word about my fantasies. "I need to get dressed for dinner."

"And?"

"And I can't until you leave my room."

"Okay, okay. For now. I won't be at dinner. Neither will Gideon. We have a business meeting in the city."

"You aren't taking Ben?"

"Sometimes. Not this time. We will be late, so I won't see you until tomorrow."

"Oh. Be careful." I turned my face and his nose touched mine. He was already leaning in to kiss me. A gentle, seductive soft play of lips and tongue that would leave me unsatisfied.

❧

I thought about Elora's lips for the length of the drive but needed to focus on the business at hand. The three of us brothers weren't getting any younger. Suddenly in the marrying mood, Gideon didn't wish to live in Thorpe manor with a new wife. While dancing at the Andrews, he overheard that our neighbor, whose land sat next to our plat, wanted to sell. It was gorgeous, wide enough for two houses and would extend the beach front of the Thorpe property. Gideon practically begged me to set up a meeting, and he didn't have to try hard to convince me. He also planned on going ring shopping first thing in the morning before we left the city to return home.

El and I were into something. I just wasn't sure yet if it was lust, love, obsession, or all three. I had never felt such a pull to another human being before, even with March. And it happened so fast. The bond forming between us worried me. What if I couldn't give my all to her? What if physical need was driving my actions? I decided to slow things down before I hurt her or myself. Even if I remained a bachelor, I had no use for the huge mansion, so I agreed to put in half with Gideon and build myself a medium sized home next to his. We both knew Ben wanted Thorpe manor, so there would be no arguing over inheritances. And Alysia practically lived at Blaine Black's home in downtown San Diego already, which our father referred to as living in sin on a daily basis. None of us would be surprised if we got word they had eloped.

❧

*M*r. Waterman walked us out of the hotel on D Street, still shaking our hands. The meeting went perfectly, and the man was in a merry mood acquiring new money.

"Gentleman, the night is young. I think I'll head over to the Canary Cottage if you'd like to join? My treat," he said, winking at us both. Now, I won't lie. I had been to the pale-yellow house with a quaint white picket fence a time...or maybe two. Once with Gideon, but that was before I met March, and he was itching to lose his virginity. I figured it was as good a place as any. The women working there were taken care of by Doc Brown to ensure the safety of their patrons.

"That is a tempting offer Mr. Waterman, but Gideon here is proposing to his girl in the next few days, and I don't think it would sit right in his mind if we participated tonight. But we do appreciate the quick meeting and look forward to finalizing the deal next week."

Gideon looked relieved I had declined, and we bid the gentleman goodbye as we stepped back inside the U.S. Grant Hotel for a drink and then sleep.

৻৵

I slept longer than Gideon who was up at dawn. He had already procured two cups of hot, steaming coffee and brought them back to our room. I welcomed the wake-up call, blinking against the sunlight. He was in a fine mood, excited to get the perfect ring, so I adjusted my own attitude, and we headed over to the marketplace across the street.

People mingled on the sidewalk, mostly window shopping. Gideon peered through a store front at shiny gold and gems. My eyebrows went up at some of the prices displayed. I was glad to be the oldest. My mother gave me our grandmother's engagement ring a few years ago, and luckily March's grandmother had insisted she wear hers. It was a small comfort knowing my family ring wasn't buried in the Andrews' family plot.

I felt a new presence beside me, too close to be another shopper, and turned to Dr. Cameron Hawkins, whose face showed no sign of the charming smile he usually wore. I gave a polite smile as did Gideon when he saw him.

A peculiar tension hung in the air, and I kept my demeanor guarded. "Cameron."

48

"Asher. Gideon. How is your family? Well, I hope?"

Gideon, still in a good mood, revealed our plans. "We're looking at engagement rings!"

Cameron got red in the face and didn't hide his frustration. He took a breath and spoke words he would soon come to regret.

"Well, that tart. She got her claws into you too, Asher? She's a wild one. Is she good on her back?"

I watched the good doctor's head fly back from the punch. I didn't even remember cocking back to hit the bastard. He remained on his feet and quickly connected a fist to my right eye. Cameron could fight, but now it was two on one as Gideon shoved him down to the ground and pummeled his face. I pulled him off after a several blows. I knew Cameron was done. He couldn't take us both on and shuffled away as fast as he could get to his feet.

I patted my bleeding temple with a handkerchief while I waited outside for Gideon. We didn't want to look like a couple of brawling Stingarees to the jeweler. It had been years since my last fight. My knuckles throbbed as I lit a cigarette and thought about life before any of the women came and changed everything. I guess that's what life was about, changing, moving forward, but I had been just fine before Elora Bannon made my whole being ache. I mean, I was grumpy and possibly depressed, but I was just fine. It would be good to get out of the manor, have a home of my own. Then I wouldn't have to hear all of the drama from the rest of them. Gideon bounced out next to me smiling like a mule over his new purchase.

"Get a good one?"

"Oh, I found a dandy. How's that eye?" He winced at me. "Ouch."

"I'll live. Let's get you back to your girl."

CHAPTER 11

*A*lysia, Mary, and I were all quietly creating when Gideon waltzed in, grabbed my cousin around the waist, and kissed her passionately right in front of us. Mary just barely tried to push him away, but he didn't let go.

"Would you go for a stroll with me?"

"Right this minute?"

"Yes. Right this minute!"

He couldn't contain his glee and whisked her down the hall and out on the portico. Alysia and I followed to spy on them. If he wanted privacy, he should have gone farther away from the house.

We jumped when Ben poked both of us in the back. "What are you two up to?"

"It's Gideon and Mary." I pointed out of the window. "He has a very small box in his hand behind his back."

Alysia squealed and squeezed Ben's hand. "Oh, it's happening!"

And then he went down on one knee and presented the open box to Mary who fell to her knees and tackled him.

❧

I didn't see Asher anywhere. The house sat quiet except for near the dining room where the others gathered to fawn over the shiny new diamond ring. I made my way to the library. He wasn't there either, but I stayed and ambled along the shelves, absently rubbing my fingers over the spines of the books.

Heavy footsteps made me turn my head as Asher stepped into the room and closed the door behind him. I leaned against the bookcase with a smile. As he came closer, I could see the fresh cut at the corner of his right eye. The lid was puffy. I reached out to soothe him, but he stopped me. His hand wrapped around my wrist.

"It's fine."

"What happened?"

He didn't answer and I felt a change in him. The back of his swollen knuckles of his free hand skimmed the warm soft curve of my breast as he held the pearl pendant hanging around my neck. My heart thudded against those long fingers. My lips yearned for his. The look in his eyes reflected anger but it made me want him more, to ease the storm inside. I didn't even care if he got rough with me. My body wanted his beyond reason. If Asher tore the necklace from my throat, I wouldn't care. Suddenly the shadows in his eyes passed as if he realized how close we were, and both hands dropped to his side.

A locked safe with the most complicated combination. That described Asher perfectly and I wondered if I would ever crack his code. Maybe I wasn't enough. Maybe he saw me as a wild thing to play with but not worth the investment of genuinely caring for or loving. My heart told me something different. A broken man stood before me. All male, all pride, and all I ever wanted.

"Ash," I desperately pleaded.

To my surprise, he turned on his heel and stomped out the door, his boots echoing through the hall.

❧

*A*fter gathering up the shattered pieces of my emotions, I found everyone else carrying celebratory drinks out back. Gideon held the door open and I followed them. I noticed his knuckles were swollen, but he spoke before I could.

"Where did Asher go?"

I got a little moody myself. He and Gideon had obviously been punching someone or something and Gideon asking me where his impossible brother was broke me.

"How should I know," I practically yelled. "What happened today? Who did you two fight with?"

We had everyone's attention, and Ben looked concerned. "Come with me." He put an arm around my shoulders and walked me down to the beach.

"What happened? And where did he go?"

"Back downtown. For a while maybe."

I didn't care where. It was the 'for a while maybe' that had tears stinging my eyes. "What happened?"

"I think he's scared. Scared of you, himself, loss. He is afraid to have it all and lose it again."

I had no words. I didn't know how it felt. I lost my parents, but I imagine that was much different than losing your other half. "What about his eye?"

"Cameron Hawkins said some awful things about you to Ash on the street, and he and Gideon gave him a good scuffle."

So, he had protected my honor and disappeared. Ben held both of my hands. "He'll be back. He always comes back." He

53

moved a hand to tilt up my chin. "He has a good reason to. You are kind, beautiful, funny…I know I wouldn't be able to stay away."

He let go of me, took a step back, and nervously ran his hands through his hair. "Sorry. I have to stop telling you everything I'm thinking. But I know Asher and he cares deeply."

I stepped in and hugged Ben hard. He was my best friend here. We spoke freely with each other. "We better go back to the others. They will start to gossip about us next," I joked. I went back in alone and wrote a letter to Lety.

❧

*M*y stomach turned as I sat on the edge of the bed in my hotel room. My own body told me it was a mistake to leave like that. My heart ached but my mind warned against falling again. It had all been too fast. Elora was swept into my life by the ocean I loved so much. It had betrayed me. Ben tried to talk me out of escaping when he caught me loading my bag into the car. So young and green. He had no idea how deep affections could cut or how big the scars were that remained mostly hidden inside.

I planned on staying in the city a while. I had to finalize the land purchase next week anyway. Maybe a few rounds of poker with the other men in town would occupy my mind instead of El.

CHAPTER 12

I couldn't will myself to sleep. It felt like I tossed and turned for hours and finally threw the quilt off with a huff. As my mind mulled over the situation, I became less heartbroken. Anger replaced the sadness and I cursed myself for falling for Asher so quickly. I left my room and tiptoed down past the vacant library, past the back doors, past the dining room and toward the kitchen to smell that familiar sweet bread baking. Mrs. Crantz leaned over a butcher block audibly reading the newspaper by lamplight, her voice low but pleasant. Liz stood peeling potatoes and noticed me but didn't acknowledge my presence. As I drew closer, I saw a woman in a wheelchair listening. It had to be Mrs. Thorpe. I paused before she noticed as her back was to me, but Mrs. Crantz saw. To my surprise she smiled, showing the lack of a couple of teeth, and motioned me to come nearer. I wrapped my shawl tight around my shoulders and stopped next to her. Mrs. Thorpe looked me up and down and grinned with a pretty, wide mouth that mirrored Asher's. He definitely took after his mother. She reached out a hand and I gave her mine.

"Well, well. You are beautiful. Mr. Thorpe told me you were."

She kept my hand in her soft one. "It is my honor to meet you Mrs. Thorpe. I've been wanting to thank you for allowing me to visit your lovely home. Alysia is brilliant and I've already learned so much."

"Oh, dear, please call me Maggie. Would you like to take some tea with me? I am a bit of a night owl. Always have been."

"I would be delighted. I can't seem to sleep either."

Mrs. Crantz busied herself putting a kettle on the stove and Maggie continued. She had a lot to say.

"You know, I used to sneak out after the house settled down for the night while the moon shined high and bright and let the cold sand sift between my toes. The wind tangled my hair and I felt at one with the ocean."

I actually had tears in my eyes. She must miss it so. "Oh, Maggie. Can I write that down in my journal? It's the prettiest thing I've ever heard."

She nodded. "Of course." Mrs. Crantz handed out the tea to Maggie and me as we enjoyed each other's company. I loved talking with her. We had so much in common. She reminded me of Aunt Rhoda.

"Do you venture out and about often late at night?" I asked.

"I do. It's the only time no one makes a fuss over me. Mrs. Crantz reads me the news and sometimes pushes me out on the portico for some fresh air."

"Oh, I would love to join you again sometime. Back home, I liked to go night swimming. Do you think anyone would notice?"

She winked and whispered, "I used to do that too."

"Well, I may have to sneak out soon then. I better return

to my room and at least try to sleep. I am so thankful to meet you. Goodnight."

❧

*I*t felt nice to spend time with the lady of the manor and know that she wasn't an invalid with no idea of the goings on of the house. She was a free spirit like me, and she didn't judge others. I wanted to ask her about Asher but decided to spend more time getting to know her first and do so without Liz around.

I was tempted to go out the back door for a swim under the stars but decided to save that for another night.

❧

*T*he medium sized club room at the U.S. Grant was packed with gentleman sitting around tables or bellied up to the bar, as it had been the three previous nights. This night, however, I spotted a familiar face keeping questionable company with a few men from Stingaree. Cameron nodded across the room and I squeezed in at the bar. When some space opened up, I was surprised to find him by my side. I lit a cigar, not looking at him when I spoke.

"I don't want any trouble."

"I'm not looking for any."

"What do you want then?"

"Let's walk. The fountain is less crowded."

I obliged and let him begin the interrogation as I kept a straight, uncaring face. Spending a decent amount of time downtown had taught me to keep a cool head and blend in.

"For a newly engaged man, you're spending a lot of time away from your fiancée, aren't you? Or did she turn you down?" He pulled out a pipe, lit it, and took a draw.

"Is any of this your business?"

"By the way you've been dragging around here, she spurned you. Am I wrong?"

"Believe me when I say you have no idea what you're talking about. I shouldn't have to explain myself to you, but it was Gideon who bought a ring that day. Certainly not me." Now I took a drag.

"Well, excuse me for assuming. The way you danced with Elora, I thought you were on the make."

"You thought wrong, but I knocked your block for being a cadet."

"I'm not a man after young girls. I desire a wildcat and I thought Elora a free spirit. Sailing alone? Women are so proper and innocent. My tastes are, shall we say, on the darker side."

I knew exactly what he meant. It explained why he hadn't married yet. It's hard to find a woman who enjoyed cruelty under the guise of pleasure, or love for that matter.

"Well, good luck with that venture. Just leave Ms. Bannon out of it. She comes from old money and a respectable family. We wouldn't want to sully that, now would we?"

He only nodded. "Is it Ben that's interested then?"

"Cameron…"

A sudden, sharp, slicing pain through the back of my left shoulder had me gasping and I watched Cameron double over as a man, one of the Stingarees I noticed earlier, appeared to sock him in the stomach, but when the man ran away with his accomplice who jerked a blade back out of my wound, Cameron's hand was bloody. Stabbed! We'd been stabbed. Pain seared down my left arm, but I fumbled with Cameron's shirt to see how bad it was. He was panting and in a bit of a shock but otherwise okay. "Just a cut. It will be okay," he said. "Asher, you're bleeding. A lot. Let's get to the Canary. It's the closest doctor."

I stumbled. My body wouldn't cooperate. Cameron swung my other arm around his shoulders and hauled me down the street. He dropped me at the stoop and went up on the porch to bang on the door. A large brute of a man answered.

"We need Doc Brown!"

"He ain't here, Dr. Hawkins."

"Then let me use his office. He'll have everything I need. And get me a blanket. I don't want to bloody up your porch getting my friend in here."

I passed out before they carried my limp body over the threshold.

CHAPTER 13

*F*our days. Four long days and even longer nights with no word from Asher. I had put down my paintbrushes and pencils to write. I wrote poetry. The words came easy. From confusion, sadness, need, secret desires, and dreams. My dreams had been vivid and sexual. When I wasn't dreaming, my nights included swimming alone and sneaking to the kitchen to visit with my new friends.

Late October brought cooler weather, so my swimming would be coming to an end. I didn't wish to be sick again. I had been trying to convince Mrs. Thorpe to join everyone in the library after dinner each night, and I could tell I was wearing her down.

One evening, about an hour before time to dine, I made my way to her room and knocked on the door. To my surprise, Ben answered.

"Elora. Hi. What? What are you doing here? Did ya get lost?"

Maggie wheeled herself over, almost hitting his ankles with her chair. "Oh, hello my friend. Won't you join us? Ben, let her in."

"Oh, well okay."

His confused look was priceless. They had been playing cards. The deck lay strewn on the game table along with tea for two and some delicious looking tarts. A kitten played with the loose strings of the quilt on her bed. I was thrilled. "A kitten! I love cats! We have cats at home." I scooped up the fluffy black ball and he nuzzled and purred under my chin. Ben scratched the tiny feline's back.

"So, you've obviously been introduced to my mother."

"Yes. And who is this?" I kissed the precious fuzzy head."

"Malachi."

Maggie reached out and I handed him over. "This is my little trouble-maker. Since Ben is all grown up, I needed another one."

"Very funny, Mother." He rolled his eyes at me. "So, when did the two of you get together?"

I didn't want to tattle on Maggie's late-night adventures, so I let her speak.

"Oh, you know I like to stay up past my bedtime. We sort of ran into each other one evening."

So, he already knew of her unusual schedule. It made me happy to see she didn't stay all cooped up alone in her room all day. I should have known Ben would be the one taking care.

"I've been trying to get Maggie to join us after dinner. Don't you agree she would be very well entertained?"

"Well, yes. I wish you would, Mother."

Maggie softened. "I guess I could for a few minutes."

Ben almost shouted a hoot. "Yes! The others won't believe it."

Mr. Thorpe flew from the other room. "What's all the commotion? Oh," he said when he saw all of us. "Did we hear from Asher?"

My heart sank at the mention of his name. Ben touched my elbow when my smile faded.

"No, Father. Mother is going to sit in the library after dinner."

Her eyebrows raised and she wagged a finger. "Only for a little while."

A genuine smile crept across his face. "Wonderful!"

&.

I played Five Card Stud with Mary, Gideon, and Ben. Maggie laughed as we teased each other. She sat by the Victrola holding Alysia's hand. Mr. Thorpe stoked the fire before retiring for the night. He kissed his wife on the forehead and took his leave.

&.

*T*he next afternoon, we took lunch out to the beach. I sat on a blanket next to Ben. My mood had been terrible at breakfast. Everyone had noticed and Alysia suggested we get out in the fresh air. The weather was perfect, and she and Gideon wanted to fish. I wasn't hungry and sat brooding. Ben put an arm around my shoulder.

"Elora, you need to eat something. You hardly touched your food this morning."

I sighed. "I don't want anything. You can have my share." I tried to lighten up, but suddenly a wave of sadness came over me and I cried. I looked away, but he noticed and pulled me closer. "I would go looking for him if you said the word."

"Oh, Ben, am I a fool? You know Asher better than anyone. Should I stop caring? Forget about him?"

"I pray you don't. In the short time you've been here, he has changed. I've seen glimpses of the old Ash. He smiles without it seeming painful. He genuinely laughs again. He danced! And the way he looks at you…"

"Well, if that is true, it sure seemed easy for him to leave."

"He never looked at March Andrews the way he looks at you. Just give him some more time. Please. Just a little."

I was unsure of what to say so I only nodded and watched Gideon reel in a piece of seaweed. Mary laughed and he threw the pole down on the sand and chased after her. The two were very much in love. All they had needed was a little push. He fell on top of her on a blanket and kissed her deeply. My body tingled thinking about Asher's lips on mine.

❧

*W*e had gathered up and started making our way back, almost reaching the back steps when Mr. Thorpe called the family to gather in the parlor. He looked troubled and I immediately knew in my heart it had something to do with Asher. I couldn't sit down and stood by the back windows where I could focus on the ocean.

"I have received a telegram from Dr. Cameron Hawkins…" His voice broke just a bit. "Oh, I'll just read it."

❧

I am sending word to inform you of an attack on Asher and myself which took place three nights ago. We were surprised outside of the U.S. Grant and both sustained injuries. Mine were minor. Asher's was and remains serious. He was stabbed from the rear into his shoulder. If left alone, he would have bled out. I found the major artery that had been severed and sewed it up as quickly as possible. Asher was very near hypovolemic shock.

He is still weak, and I have continued dressing changes. If gangrene sets in, the limb could be lost, or worse, a systemic infection could result in death. Please know the wound appears to be clean, he is in the very best of care and being kept comfortably sedated. I insistently request that you resist the urge to visit. It is of the utmost importance. He is in isolation so as to stave off the transfer of germs. I will be in contact again soon with an update.

&.

*T*here were gasps and tears. I had so many questions, as did everyone.

CHAPTER 14

*D*arkness and El. All I saw was her face. All I wanted was to see her, touch her, hold her close, tell her I was an idiot. Reality seeped in through a drug induced haze, and I blinked against the light coming through the window, wincing at the pain in my shoulder. When I was truly aware of where I was and what had happened, Cameron explained why we were so suddenly attacked. In classic Cameron fashion, he had propositioned the wrong girl. A married woman who worked at the local bakery. Her husband along with his brother were the two who accosted us.

"You must rest Asher. I will send an update to your family, but you have to rest," Cameron said sternly.

"No. Don't just yet. I don't want them coming here and seeing me like this."

"Very well. Now that you are awake, you should gain strength pretty fast. We will get you up walking tomorrow. You haven't been able to eat much besides liquids, so I'll get you a real meal. I'll be back shortly."

"Thank you."

I realized I was starving. I scooted up in the bed and pulled down the covers a little to see my flat stomach. I could tell I had lost a few pounds. My face was covered in scruff as well.

A beautiful blonde came into my room carrying a tray. I assumed she performed a very different job here after dark. She spoke with a pretty, Irish accent.

"Hello, Mr. Thorpe. Dr. Hawkins said you were awake, so I brought ya fresh coffee. I'll change your dressin' after you have your fill." She placed the bed tray over my lap and sat in the chair beside the bed.

"Have you been taking care of me?"

She smiled. "Yes. We wanted to keep as many germs out as we could, so Dr. Hawkins and I, I'm Beth, are the only ones who are allowed in. I feed you soup mostly and bathe you and apply clean bandages to your wound. It is looking wonderful by the way."

I felt a little embarrassed that she had obviously seen me naked and that I had been as helpless as an infant. "I sincerely appreciate everything you've done for me." The coffee tasted like heaven, and I groaned.

She giggled. "Is it that good?"

"Oh yes. I guess I've missed it."

Cameron walked in with a brown bag that smelled like baked bread and grilled steak and my stomach growled. The two watched as I devoured it all then Beth proceeded to tend to my shoulder.

I spoke to Cameron, "Do you think I could get a shaving cup and a razor? I can do it myself."

"Of course. I'll get you a new suit. It's the least I can do. All of this is my fault. I am sorry things went south."

I only nodded. He was right and I wasn't about to become best friends with the cad. Beth finished and Cameron stood to leave.

"I have to see a few patients in town. Beth can get your razor and I'll be back with supper and new clothes."

ૐ

I felt more like myself after a shave and Cameron spent a good penny on the new suit as well as a couple of regular slacks and shirts. I couldn't wait to see Elora. I owed her a huge apology, but I needed to get my strength back before I went home.

ૐ

S itting on the rock where Asher and I kissed and watching the ocean had replaced my late-night swimming. Worry, sadness, and despair at the thought of losing him cycled through my mind, eventually transitioning to anger remembering how he made me fall for him before he vanished. He could be dead for all I knew, and my heart broke again.

Surely Cameron would let us know if Asher's condition deteriorated or would he be scared and run, thinking the family held him responsible? Tears ceased to come anymore. I had none left to give. I spent more and more time alone in my room after sketching or painting in the mornings. Alysia and Mary eventually stopped trying to console me and Ben distanced himself but sat food outside my door whenever I skipped lunch or dinner. I forced myself to eat just so I wouldn't get sick. The house fell quiet.

CHAPTER 15

*A*s soon as I walked in, Ben practically knocked me down. He had watched the glowing head lamps travel down the driveway.

"Ash, I thought you were dead. We all did."

I pulled him away to see his face. "I know and I'm sorry for that. I couldn't return until I was back to myself."

Everyone else heard the commotion and gathered around me except Elora. I hugged each of them and profusely apologized.

"I feel so lucky to be alive. If…" and then I cried. Tears rolled down my cheeks in front of the family I had come to appreciate more than ever.

"Never mind that, son. Just don't ever leave us like that again." Dad held my face with both hands.

I wiped my sleeve across my face and glanced around. "Where is she?"

Mother grabbed my hand. "Elora is in her room. She hasn't been herself. She's angry and I don't blame her. Why don't you go out for a moment, calm yourself and Ben can tell her you are home?"

I nodded, stepped outside, and went down the steps to feel the sand.

❧

A knock on the door made me jump. "Yes?"
"It's me."

Ben. I welcomed him. He understood me better than anyone in the house. He searched my face and grabbed my shoulders. "Elora, Ash is back."

My tired eyes went wide. A thrill rumbled through me along with a nervous energy I couldn't place. I had truly mourned his loss. Now Asher was alive, and he had returned. I didn't know what it meant yet, but in that moment, I forgave him. I knew I loved him. I wanted to tell him. I embraced Ben tightly. "Oh, thank heavens."

I broke away and tried to tame my hair. "Where is he? Does he want to see me?"

Ben smiled. "Very much. Mother knows how hurt you've been and told him to step outside. I'll go get him."

"No, I'll go find him."

I ran downstairs and into the middle of the rest of the family. I threw my shawl on the sofa before Mary caught my arm. "Wait. We can call him in."

"No, I need to talk to him alone."

I stepped out onto the portico while they watched after me from the windows. When I reached the top step, I saw his face looking up at mine from the bottom and I froze. Our eyes locked for a few moments and every particle in my body felt on edge, wondering what words I would hear him utter. Then that wide mouth smiled and parted as if he had no words. He slowly took each step up closer to where I waited. As soon as he came within reach, his arms went around my waist and his head pressed into my stomach, holding me so tight.

"El," he mumbled into my tummy. "I love you."

He pulled back but didn't let me go. I couldn't stop touching him. His face, his hair, his shoulders. He was alive and he loved me. I couldn't disconnect.

"I thought you were gone."

"El, can you ever forgive me?"

I pulled him up onto the portico, still holding on, and he looked down at me.

"I love you. I love you but if you ever leave me like that again, I won't be here when you get back."

"Never. Never again," he growled and then kissed me. His arms held me around my waist, and he lifted me from my feet and twirled me around.

"Your arm!"

"It's fine. Just a little weak and sore. I'll be fine…as long as I have you. I wasn't sure if you would still be here. When I woke up, all I wanted was to see your face. To tell you…that I want you. I need you. If you'll have me. I want to marry you. I don't want to live if I don't have you."

I showered kisses over his handsome face, then his lips. Those lips that were all mine. Asher Thorpe was mine and I would marry him that instant if he wanted.

"El, is that a yes?"

"Yes. Yes!"

He pressed so hard against me and I needed him.

"El, come with me now. Stay with me tonight. I don't care what anyone thinks. I'm all yours and I need to feel you. I don't want to be apart."

My body burned at his words.

We entered hand in hand and when the others started to speak, Asher barked, "Tomorrow. We can hash it all out tomorrow. I need to speak with Elora in private. Don't disturb us." He pulled me down the long hall into his room and locked the door with a loud click.

He took off his coat and sat on the green velvet sofa, tugging me onto his lap. I curled up as close as I could physically get, and he held me, nuzzling my neck with his nose, breathing in my scent as I kept a hand on his heart to know he was actually there. When he kissed my neck with soft gentle lips, my hands slid to the buttons of his shirt. I shifted and repositioned, sliding my skirt up so I could straddle him, and he helped get his shirt the rest of the way off. I leaned closer, my long hair falling across his chest, and my fingers found the fresh scar on the back of Asher's shoulder. I traced around it and he let out a sigh. His hands were under my skirt on my thighs and I was wet with want. I shimmied my dress over my head, which left me covered only by a thin peach silk chemise. Asher's gaze swept over me and I lost control. I grabbed him, kissing him into oblivion. Our hands went wild and soon we were standing and had stripped each other naked. Then we paused, looking at each other. I spoke first.

"You're really here."

"And I'm all yours. Are you mine?"

I was a candle. He was a lit match and I needed to partake of his flame. I reached down to stroke his cock and he moaned, grasped my hips, and pushed me backwards towards his bed. I pulled him down over my body and kissed him some more. More. I had to have more. I would never get enough of Asher Thorpe. He stopped and looked down at me, smiling.

"Before we…I have something for you."

Asher slid down my body, placing a kiss every few inches before leaving me sprawled on his bed naked and aching with need as he retrieved a box from the top drawer of his wardrobe. My love for Asher went far deeper than good looks, but my god, he resembled the Roman statues I had seen in one of my aunt's museum books. He lay beside me propped up on his forearms.

"This is for you, El. It's always been meant for you. It was my grandmother's."

I gasped when he opened the blue box. A large diamond as bright as a star in the night sky twinkled against the black velvet lining. Deep blue sapphires encircled the precious gem. My favorite shade of blue.

"Grandfather spoiled her. As I will you."

Asher placed the ring on my finger. It fit perfectly. He rubbed a hand across my belly then lower and I gasped again. Oh, how naughty he looked, smiling from ear to ear like he was about to swallow me whole. I tingled with excitement and need. I had imagined his hands on me from the first moment I saw him. His hand stayed put while fingers circled over and over, delightfully slow. I pulled his mouth to mine as the best sensation I had ever felt grew like a blazing fire inside. I couldn't help myself and pushed my hips harder against his hand and when my body exploded with pleasure Asher slid his fingers inside while I pulsated around them, his lips pressing into my neck, teeth nipping at my earlobe.

"El. My god. I love you. You feel so good," he growled.

"And I'm all yours, Ash. I love you. That was amazing. I've never been with anyone before, but I need you. I want to feel you."

I touched him and he moaned. I knew he needed release.

"It may hurt this time, but I don't mean to hurt you."

"I know. I have read all about it." I laughed. "I know it gets better and better."

I pulled his hips on top of mine and he took his time easing inside. He had made me so wet before, and it only stung when he had made it in all the way. I winced and he paused, searching my eyes.

"Ash, I love being this close to you." I took his bottom lip in between my teeth. "You're all mine."

He kissed me and laughed. "I have wanted to do that to you since I met you. You minx. I *am* all yours. I'm going to kiss you all night long."

He began moving in a rhythm that made me never want him to stop. "El, it's not going to take long. It has been a long time," he said in between breaths.

"I'm yours."

After a few more swift moves, his body fell heavy on top of mine and the throbbing had me clinging to him.

"Don't get up. Stay inside. I want you inside."

Tears came and I knew it was because of the immense love I felt for Asher and thinking about how I almost lost him. He raised up and wiped my cheeks. "Darling."

"Yesterday I didn't know if you were alive and tonight I have you. Here. With me."

"I meant it when I promised to never leave you again. If things hadn't worked out. I mean, if I wasn't able to make it back to you before I told you how I felt about you, I can't fathom the pain it would have caused. I'm such a scoundrel, leaving the way I did. I can't believe I treated you like that. You deserve so much more. I'm going to give you so much more."

Asher pulled the quilt over us and me to his side. I laid my ear to his heart and treasured the steady beats.

"I need to speak with Gideon, but before everything happened, we were supposed to meet with the contractor next week to go over plans to build two houses on the beach plats next to the manor. I think you should come. Our home needs to have your touch. I want you to love it."

"I would love anything you want but thank you. Ash, do we have to have a big wedding?"

"Well, the people who know me know I wouldn't care about such a thing, and as for strangers, I don't give a damn what they think. I leave it in your hands, darling. I'll do your bidding."

I smiled because we fit together so well.

"Even as a little girl I never wished for a lavish affair. I don't want to wait long either. My only desire is for Lety and your family to be present. Do you think we could simply share our vows here…on the beach?"

Asher kissed me and hugged me tighter. "It's perfect. My favorite place in the world with a few guests and the perfect woman? Nothing would make me happier. Gideon and Mary's wedding will be enough to appease the public and we can arrange ours soon so the spotlight can shine on them."

"That's just what I was thinking."

Asher rolled back on top of me. "And we will move your things into my room," he said, kissing my neck.

"Too bad it's too cold to go swimming now."

"Yes, but I can think of a few things to keep us occupied."

"Oh, I'm looking forward to it."

CHAPTER 16

*W*aking with Asher curled around me felt like a dream. His room was far enough down the hall that I couldn't tell if anyone else was stirring about the manor. I stretched a little and Asher pulled me even closer and grumbled, "No. Not yet. I've never had anyone in my bed, and it feels so good. I may keep you here."

"Forever?"

"Mmm, yes forever."

"It's so tempting, but we wouldn't ever see the beach again or dance or swim…"

He propped up on one arm and kissed my nose. "Oh, alright. I am getting hungry. I didn't have any supper last night." He reached for his watch on the bedside table. "We should be just in time for breakfast."

*A*fter stopping in my room to change, we joined the family in the dining room. Everyone was present except Maggie. They all smiled and told Asher how glad they were to have him back. We sat next to one another across from Mary and Gideon and my ring caught her eye.

"Oh my gosh, Elora! Do you two have some news, or are you going to make us all wonder?"

Asher spoke up. "El and I *are* engaged, but we have decided to have a very small, very simple ceremony right here on the beach after Lety arrives. Neither one of us wants a grand affair and we just can't wait." He leaned over and kissed my temple while the others shared their joy and congratulations.

"Yes. And then we are planning the most amazing wedding San Diego has ever seen for Gideon and Mary," I added.

Mary beamed. "I can't wait!"

"Neither can I," Gideon spoke heatedly to Mary.

❧

I prepared my room for Lety since I had moved into Asher's. The past two weeks had flown by and had been very busy with planning our small ceremony and meeting with the contractor to discuss our future home. Maggie spent more and more time with the family after Asher's return.

❧

I hugged my sister tight in front of the Southern Pacific Arcade Depot and she whispered into my ear, "Elora, he's just breathtaking" speaking of Asher who smiled and took her small trunk. She never stopped asking questions during our ride to the manor. We got back at dark, and Ben greeted us at the door. Lety's eyes lit up and I could see and feel the chemistry between them.

"Welcome Ms. Bannon. I'm so glad you came. El has told us all about you," Ben beamed.

"Oh, please call me Lety," she flirted, placing her hand on his forearm.

I was a little surprised. She did it so well. There would be no problem pushing these two together at all. Ben grabbed her things out of Asher's hand and led her to her room as I followed the pair. I practically had to shove him out of the door.

"Go on now. We will see you at breakfast."

He reluctantly said goodnight and I hugged Lety again and kissed her forehead after tucking her into bed.

꩜

I returned to Asher's room and there he sat on our bed, shirtless. My body instantly responded. He reached out. "Come here, beautiful girl."

I curled up in his lap and laid my head under his chin. "I finally have her here," I sighed. "I think Ben is more excited than I am. And did you see her batting her eyelashes at him?"

A laugh rumbled in Asher's bare chest. "She's quite different from you. You never batted your eyelashes at me."

"You would have thought me childish if I had," I scoffed. His hand that rested on my back slid to my bottom and he pulled me up to look into his eyes.

"There's nothing childish about you. I can only describe you as mesmerizing. I have all love and pure lust for you, my darling." His voice sizzled, making me burn. I moved my knee and straddled his hips to show him exactly what I wanted, and he gave it perfectly.

❧

*T*he breakfast room buzzed like a beehive. Lety and Ben talked and laughed nonstop. Maggie and I discussed the ceremony that was all set for the next day while Gideon and Mary listened. And Asher and Mr. Thorpe sat at each end of the long table, observing the whole scene. They looked very content with their enlarging family. All of us girls helped Mrs. Crantz clean up and then went to the drawing room while the men tended to business. Lety took over my easel while I wrote in my notebook.

❧

I was not surprised when Ben came in and sat next to me, throwing his arm around my shoulders. He leaned close. "Would you object to me asking your sister for an afternoon stroll after lunch?"

"Of course not."

He went to stand by her side, and she smiled but didn't look away from the canvas. His eyes roamed her body, and he had the most adoring look as he studied her profile.

"What do you think?" she asked and brought him out of his thoughts.

Her painting talent far exceeded my own and her landscape was beautiful.

"Um, well, I think it is lovely but not as lovely as the painter."

Her cheeks blushed and she turned to him. "Thank you, Ben."

I couldn't help but swoon just watching them.

He gently touched her elbow. "Lety, would you like to take a walk with me this afternoon?"

"Oh, yes. I'd love to."

The pair had me yearning for Asher, and he magically appeared in the doorway as if I had summoned him. He peeked his head in and winked at me. "Busy, darling?"

I closed my notebook and shook my head. He came to sit and pulled me onto his lap. I kissed him and heard Lety giggling. I didn't care. I wanted her to know what love should look like. Asher nuzzled my nose with his. "Tomorrow is the big day. You won't get cold-feet, will you?"

"Never, Ash."

The heat we shared permeated the room.

"Save some for tomorrow, you two," Ben teased.

❧

*E*lora decided to sleep with Lety. I reluctantly agreed it would make our wedding night special. She managed to stay away from me the entire day and my excitement built as the time came near. My emotions were getting the better of me as I thought about how lucky I was. The fateful day she washed ashore I knew I was a goner. Feeling like I didn't deserve her made me hold on tighter. I didn't need anything else in the world, and I would give the world to El if she asked.

Ben's smiling face was a welcome sight as I wiped my eyes and straightened my tie.

"It's almost time, big shot. You're the luckiest man around, you know," Ben said sincerely.

I grabbed hold of his shoulders. "Thank you. Thank you for being there for Elora when I wasn't. I love you, brother and so does El."

Ben hugged me and mumbled, "Be good to her. She's my friend." I only nodded, grateful for my family.

࿐

*T*he ceremony was perfect. The bride took my breath away and I would spend the rest of my long life loving Elora.

ACKNOWLEDGMENTS

A special thank you to my family and friends who continue to support my passion of writing.

A special shout out to those of you who read my rough drafts and offer your honest opinions. You are all priceless to me.

A great story wouldn't be as perfect as possible without an amazing editor, so a big THANK YOU goes out to Brandi Zelenka of My Notes in the Margin editing services.

ABOUT THE AUTHOR

Ginger Lee, romance novelist and dark poet, spends her days raising her daughter, traveling with her husband, and attending concerts with friends. She is an avid reader and coffee & vampire enthusiast who collects art, movies, Monster High Dolls and oddities. In her free time, she enjoys walks through the neighborhood and thrift store shopping. Ginger loves to connect with other authors, readers, and the writing community on social media.

PLAYLIST

Satellite Heart – Anya Marina
Love Me Whole – Missio
Northern Wind – City and Colour
Like I'm Gonna Lose You – Nicholas Yee
Clair de lune – Claude Debussy
Like Real People Do – Hozier
Moonlight Sonata – Ludwig van Beethoven
Make You Feel My Love – Sleeping At Last

HOW TO CONTACT GINGER LEE

- Email: gleewrites@gmail.com
- Website: gleewrites.com
- www.twitter.com/glee_writes
- www.instagram.com/authorgingerlee
- https://ko-fi.com/gingerlee
- https://allauthor.com/author/gleewrites/.
- www.goodreads.com/gleewrites
- www.facebook.com/gingerweather
- Amazon: